Sandy Creek
NEW YORK

An Imprint of Sterling Publishing
387 Park Avenue South
New York, NY 10016

This 2010 edition published by Sandy Creek,

ISBN: 978-1-4351-2658-9
Manufactured in Heshan, China
Lot #:
4 6 8 10 9 7 5
07/13

Mickey's Christmas Carol

Sandy Creek
NEW YORK

One snowy Christmas Eve, one person was not thinking about trees
or presents. His name was Ebenezer Scrooge!

Scrooge hurried past a group of carolers.

"God bless you, sir," one of them called out. "Please spare a coin
for a poor, hungry child!"

"Bah! Humbug!" replied Scrooge. "If the poor want to be rich,
let them work as hard as I do."

With his cane, Scrooge knocked the snow from the sign above his office door. He was thinking about his partner, Jacob Marley, who had passed away seven years ago that very night.

"He was a good one! He robbed the widows and swindled the poor!" Scrooge chuckled to himself.

Scrooge's clerk, Bob Cratchit, was busily working.

"It's freezing today," he thought. "Surely Scrooge won't miss one little piece of coal."

"Caught you!" Scrooge shouted, bursting into the room. "That coal costs a pretty penny, you know."

"I was just trying to thaw my ink," stammered Cratchit.

"Bah! You used a piece last week," the miserly Scrooge replied. "Now get back to work."

Old Scrooge sat down at his desk and lovingly polished his gold coins until they glowed brightly.

He weighed them on the scales and stacked them carefully on the desktop. With a quill pen, he scratched figures in an enormous book. Suddenly the door flew open with a bang.

13

"Merry Christmas!" cried Scrooge's nephew Fred, offering his uncle a wreath and an invite to Christmas dinner. "What's this? Poor Cratchit still working on Christmas Eve?"

"Bah! Humbug!" snorted Scrooge, snatching the wreath from Fred and throwing it into the fire. "We never close! Now good day to you, sir, there is work to be done."

Fred tipped his hat and left, giving Cratchit a look of pity.

"Oh, to spend Christmas Day at home," thought Cratchit as he jumped down from his stool.

"Mind you are in even earlier the day after, and don't forget my dirty laundry!" snapped Scrooge.

Cratchit nodded as he snatched up the bag of laundry and shouted "Merry Christmas!" as he left.

Scrooge locked up his office and hurried home.

"Am I seeing things? No, it couldn't be…Jacob Marley? Is that you?" gasped Scrooge, looking at his doorknocker.

The face on the door called softly, "Scrooooooge!"

Frightened, Scrooge yanked open the door, ran inside, and slammed the door behind him.

Scrooge flew up the stairs three at a time, but behind him he could hear the sound of chains clanking.

Looking over his shoulder, he froze in his tracks. It was the ghost of Marley!

Scrooge ran into his bedroom and bolted the door shut. He sank
down in his chair. He knew that no door had ever kept a ghost out
—although this ghost knocked politely before he floated in.
    "Scrooge, don't you recognize your old friend?" asked
    the ghost. "I was your partner, Jacob Marley."

Suddenly the ghost tripped over Scrooge's cane, knocked over the chair, then landed in a heap on top of it. A deafening thud shook the room as a heavy chest fell beside them.

"The real Jacob Marley was never so clumsy," said Scrooge.

"Do not mock me!" boomed the ghost. "If I am clumsy, 'tis because of these chains I must always carry with me."

"What about that chest?" exclaimed Scrooge. "Let me take a look."

"Stop!" thundered the ghost. "The chest is heavier than all the treasure in the world. All my miserable deeds are locked in here, and chained to me forever. I can never be free. I come to warn you, Scrooge. Change your ways or you are doomed! You will be visited this night by three spirits. Listen to them well, for only they can save you now."

In an instant Marley was gone.

Scrooge quickly pulled on his nightshirt and cap, and hopped into bed. A little figure appeared, wearing a top hat, holding an umbrella.

"The hour has come, Mr. Scrooge!" he called. "There is not a moment to lose."

"But-but...who are you?" croaked Scrooge.

"I am the Ghost of Christmas Past," the figure replied. "Do as I say."

"A midget!" snickered Scrooge. "You do not frighten me."

"Silence!" ordered the Spirit. "If men were measured by their kindness, you would be smaller than a grain of sand! Catch hold of me for we are going back to a time when Christmas was not humbug!"

The window flew open, and instantly Scrooge and the Spirit of Christmas Past soared over rooftops and chimneys, the Spirit's red umbrella keeping them afloat.

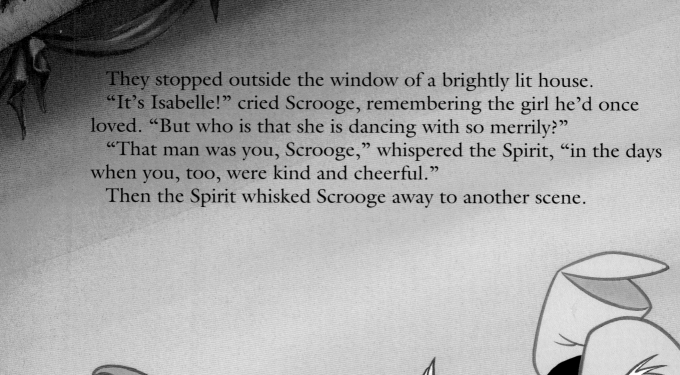

They stopped outside the window of a brightly lit house.

"It's Isabelle!" cried Scrooge, remembering the girl he'd once loved. "But who is that she is dancing with so merrily?"

"That man was you, Scrooge," whispered the Spirit, "in the days when you, too, were kind and cheerful."

Then the Spirit whisked Scrooge away to another scene.

The old Scrooge sat behind his desk laden with money. But Isabelle was crying.

"Your greed drove her away, Ebenezer," said the Spirit. "You were to marry, but you loved only money."

"I wanted us to be happy...to be rich..." moaned Scrooge.

"You left her with nothing!" accused the Spirit.

Suddenly Scrooge found himself back in bed.

"That must have been a bad dream," he thought. Then he thought of Isabelle, and how his love of money had ruined his chance of happiness with the girl he loved.

Scrooge was sobbing into his pillow when he felt a heavy hand on his shoulder.

"I am the Ghost of Christmas Present!" boomed a giant.

"Oh, please!" cried Scrooge. "Spare me."

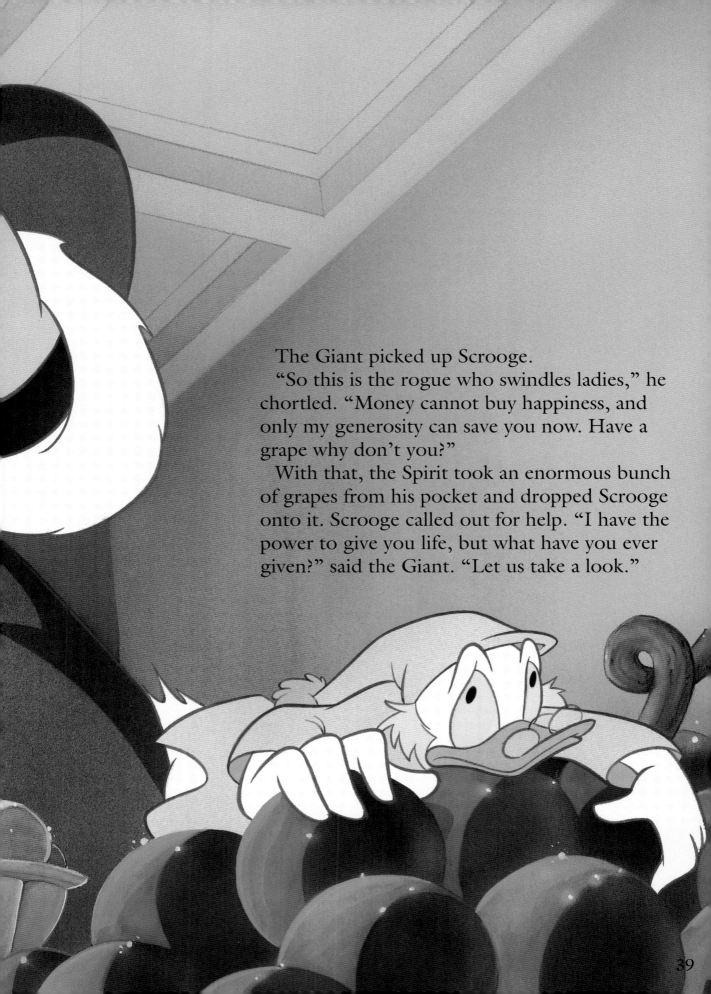

The Giant picked up Scrooge.

"So this is the rogue who swindles ladies," he chortled. "Money cannot buy happiness, and only my generosity can save you now. Have a grape why don't you?"

With that, the Spirit took an enormous bunch of grapes from his pocket and dropped Scrooge onto it. Scrooge called out for help. "I have the power to give you life, but what have you ever given?" said the Giant. "Let us take a look."

"There's no time to lose," the Spirit cried, scooping up Scrooge. He pushed open the roof and stepped out.

In seconds the spirit and Scrooge had arrived at a tiny, run-down house.

"What a dreadful little house!" exclaimed Scrooge, looking in the window. "There's Bob Cratchit! Does he live here?"

The spirit scowled. "Look how he lives, thanks to your generosity! Look at the food his family will eat this Christmas Eve."

The hungry Cratchit family were about to eat the smallest goose Scrooge had ever seen.

"What is in that huge pot on the stove?" he commented.

"Your laundry!" said the Spirit.

A small boy hobbled into the room, leaning on a little crutch.

"That is Tiny Tim," replied the Spirit. "He is very sick. He must have good food every day to make him well again."

When Scrooge stepped back from the window, the Spirit had disappeared. A smoky haze hung in the air.

"H-E-L-P!" he called. "Don't leave me here…Come back!"

Suddenly, Scrooge sneezed so hard that he went flying through the air, then landed in soft snow near some tombstones.

But Scrooge was no longer alone. A horrible spectre stood silently before him.

Scrooge saw what had made him sneeze: A gigantic cigar glowed in the Spirit's horrible mouth.

Suddenly, the spirit spoke.

"I am the Ghost of Christmas Yet to Come. Who are you looking for in this lonely place?"

"Please sir, help me find Tiny Tim," begged Scrooge. Very slowly the Spirit raised his hand and pointed to a tombstone.

Scrooge looked, and saw Bob
Cratchit placing Tiny Tim's little
crutch on a grave. Tears rolled
down Cratchit's face.

Scrooge's heart sank. He wanted
to say how sorry he was, when
suddenly a bell began to toll.

Scrooge turned away, tears in his eyes. Then he saw another grave gaping in front of him.

"Wh-whose lonely grave is this?" he asked the Ghost of Christmas Yet to Come.

"Why, yours, Ebenezer," laughed the Spirit, lighting another cigar.

"Oh, please!" cried Scrooge. "I'm so sorry! Tell me these events can yet be changed!"

But the Spirit just laughed and slapped Scrooge on the back.

"H-e-e-e-l-p!" screamed Scrooge, as he went flying into the pit.

As he fell, he remembered all the people he had robbed and swindled in the past. "I'll change! Let me out! Let me…"

Suddenly another bell was ringing.

Scrooge opened his eyes, jumped out of bed and ran to the window. The sun shone brightly. It was Christmas morning.

"But, but, if it is still Christmas morning," stammered Scrooge, "what the Spirit showed me last night has not yet happened. Tiny Tim still lives!"

Scrooge threw on his hat and coat, and ran outside.

"Merry Christmas!" the carolers called to Scrooge.

"And a Merry Christmas to you!" replied Scrooge as he pushed gold coins in their hands.

"Merry Christmas, Fred!" Scrooge cried to his nephew. "I've no time to stop, but don't start dinner without me! There's just one thing I must do."

Fred was so surprised at his uncle's cheerfulness, he almost fell off his carriage.

Scrooge knocked on Bob Cratchit's door, with a big brown sack on his back.

"As you're not working today, I've brought a sack of dirty laundry," said Scrooge. "See that it's done today!"

"Oh! Look!" cried Tiny Tim's sister as Scrooge walked past. "Isn't that a teddy bear in Mr. Scrooge's sack?"

Scrooge threw the sack on the floor.

"Open it!" he cried.

Parcels tied with bright ribbons and bows tumbled from the sack.

"There are more surprises, children," chuckled Scrooge. "Look at the marvelous goose, and there are chestnuts, and even a Christmas pudding! What a Christmas you shall have. A very Merry Christmas to you all, and especially to you, Tiny Tim!

The whole family danced with joy. This was to be the first of many bountiful holidays, for they would never be poor again. Cratchit was to become Scrooge's new partner, and Tiny Tim wouldn't go hungry, and would grow stronger each day.

"How good it is to be generous and kind!" thought Ebenezer Scrooge.

"God bless us, every one," said Tiny Tim.